Books by Roald Dahl

THE BFG
BILLY AND THE MINPINS
BOY: TALES OF CHILDHOOD
BOY *and* GOING SOLO
CHARLIE AND THE CHOCOLATE FACTORY
CHARLIE AND THE GREAT GLASS ELEVATOR
THE COMPLETE ADVENTURES OF CHARLIE AND MR WILLY WONKA
DANNY THE CHAMPION OF THE WORLD
THE ENORMOUS CROCODILE
ESIO TROT
FANTASTIC MR FOX
GEORGE'S MARVELLOUS MEDICINE
THE GIRAFFE AND THE PELLY AND ME
GOING SOLO
JAMES AND THE GIANT PEACH
MATILDA
THE MAGIC FINGER
THE TWITS
THE WITCHES

Picture books

DIRTY BEASTS
THE ENORMOUS CROCODILE
THE GIRAFFE AND THE PELLY AND ME
THE MINPINS
REVOLTING RHYMES

Plays

THE BFG: THE PLAYS (*Adapted by David Wood*)
[CHARL]IE AND THE CHOCOLATE FACTORY: THE PLAY (*Adapted by Richard George*)
[DANN]Y THE CHAMPION OF THE WORLD: THE PLAYS (*Adapted by David Wood*)
FANTASTIC MR FOX: THE PLAY (*Adapted by Sally Reid*)
[JA]MES AND THE GIANT PEACH: THE PLAY (*Adapted by Richard George*)
THE TWITS: THE PLAYS (*Adapted by David Wood*)
THE WITCHES: THE PLAYS (*Adapted by David Wood*)

Teenage fiction

[THE GR]EAT AUTOMATIC GRAMMATIZATOR AND OTHER STORIES
RHYME STEW
SKIN AND OTHER STORIES
THE VICAR OF NIBBLESWICKE
[THE W]ONDERFUL STORY OF HENRY SUGAR AND SIX MORE

Collections

THE ROALD DAHL TREASURY
SONGS AND VERSE

D1145293

BILLY and the
MINPINS

ROALD DAHL

BILLY and the MINPINS

Illustrated by *Quentin Blake*

PUFFIN

PUFFIN BOOKS

UK | USA | Canada | Ireland | Australia
India | New Zealand | South Africa

Puffin Books is part of the Penguin Random House group of companies
whose addresses can be found at global.penguinrandomhouse.com.

www.penguin.co.uk   www.puffin.co.uk   www.ladybird.co.uk

Penguin
Random House
UK

First published as *The Minpins* by Jonathan Cape 1991
Published by Puffin Books 1993
Published as *Billy and the Minpins* 2017

001

Text copyright © Roald Dahl Nominee Ltd, 1991
Illustrations copyright © Quentin Blake, 2017

The moral right of the author and illustrator has been asserted

Typeset in Baskerville MT Std
Printed in Great Britain by Clays Ltd, St Ives plc

A CIP catalogue record for this book is available from the British Library

ISBN: 978–0–141–37750–6

All correspondence to:
Puffin Books
Penguin Random House Children's
80 Strand, London WC2R ORL

MIX
Paper from
responsible sources
FSC   FSC® C018179
www.fsc.org

Penguin Random House is committed to a
sustainable future for our business, our readers
and our planet. This book is made from Forest
Stewardship Council® certified paper.

For Ophelia

CONTENTS

Being Good

Little Billy's mother was always telling him exactly what he was allowed to do and what he was not allowed to do.

All the things he was allowed to do were boring. All the things he was not allowed to do were exciting.

One of the things he was NEVER NEVER allowed to do, the most exciting of them all, was to go out through the garden gate all by himself and explore the world beyond.

On this sunny summer afternoon, Little Billy was kneeling on a chair in the living room, gazing out through the window at the wonderful world beyond. His mother was in the kitchen doing the ironing and although the door was open she couldn't see him.

Every now and again his mother would call out to him, saying, 'Little Billy, what are you up to in there?'

And Little Billy would always call back and say, 'I'm being good, Mummy.'

But Little Billy was awfully tired of being good.

Through the window, not so very far away, he could see the big black secret wood that was called The Forest of Sin. It was something he had always longed to explore.

His mother had told him that even grown-ups were frightened of going into The Forest of Sin.

She recited a poem to him that was well known in the district. It went like this:

Beware! Beware! The Forest of Sin!
None come out, but many go in!

'Why don't they come out?' Little Billy asked her. 'What happens to them in the wood?'

'That wood,' his mother said, 'is full of the most bloodthirsty wild beasts in the world.'

'You mean tigers and lions?' Little Billy asked.

'Much worse than that,' his mother said.

'What's worse than tigers and lions, Mummy?'

'Whangdoodles are worse,' his mother said, 'and Hornswogglers and Snozzwanglers and Vermicious Knids.

And worst of all is the Terrible Bloodsuckling Toothpluckling Stonechuckling Spittler. There's one of them in there, too.'

'A Spittler, Mummy?'

'Of course. And when the Spittler chases after you, he blows clouds of hot smoke out of his nose.'

'Would he eat me up?' Little Billy asked.

'In one gulp,' his mother said.

Little Billy did not believe a word of this. He guessed his mother was making it all up just to frighten him and stop him ever going out of the house alone.

And now Little Billy was kneeling on the chair, gazing with longing through the window at the famous Forest of Sin.

'Little Billy,' his mother called out from the kitchen. 'What are you doing?'

'I'm being good, Mummy,' Little Billy called back.

Just then a funny thing happened. Little Billy began to hear somebody whispering in his ear. He knew exactly who it was. It was the Devil. The Devil always started whispering to him when he was especially bored.

'It would be easy,' the Devil was whispering, 'to climb out through that window. No one would see you. And in a jiffy you would be in the garden, and in another jiffy you would be through the front gate, and in yet another jiffy you would be exploring the marvellous Forest of Sin all by yourself. It is a super place. Do not believe one word of what your mother says about Whangdoodles and Hornswogglers and Snozzwanglers and Vermicious Knids and the Terrible Bloodsuckling Toothpluckling Stonechuckling Spittler. There are no such things.'

'What *is* in there?' Little Billy whispered.

'Wild strawberries,' the Devil whispered back. 'The whole floor of the forest is carpeted with wild strawberries, every one of them luscious and red and juicy-ripe. Go and see for yourself.'

These were the words the Devil whispered softly into Little Billy's ear on that sunny summer afternoon.

The next moment, Little Billy had opened the window and was climbing out.

Run, Little Billy!
Run Run Run!

In a jiffy Little Billy had dropped silently on to the flowerbed below.

In another jiffy he was out through the garden gate.

And in yet another jiffy he was standing on the very edge the great big dark Forest of Sin!

He had made it! He had got there! And now the forest was all his to explore!

Was he nervous?

What?

Who said anything about being nervous?

Hornswogglers? Vermicious Knids? What sort of rubbish was that?

Little Billy hesitated.

'I'm not nervous,' he said. 'I'm not in the least bit nervous. Not me.'

Very very slowly, he walked into the great forest. Giant trees were soon surrounding him on all sides and their branches made an almost solid roof high above his head, blotting out the sky. Here and there little shafts of sunlight shone through gaps in the roof. There was not a sound anywhere. It was like being among the dead men in an enormous empty green cathedral.

When he had ventured some distance into the forest, Little Billy stopped and stood quite still, listening. He could hear nothing. Nothing at all. There was absolute silence.

Or was there?

Hold on just one second.

What was that?

Little Billy flicked his head round and stared into the everlasting gloom and doom of the forest.

There it was again! There was no mistaking it this time.

From far away, there came a very faint whoozing whiffling noise, like a small gusty wind blowing through the trees.

Then it grew louder. Every second it was growing louder, and suddenly it was no longer a small wind, it was a fearsome swooshing whooshing whiffling snorting noise that sounded as though some gigantic creature was breathing heavily through its nose as it galloped towards him.

Little Billy turned and ran.

Little Billy ran faster than he had ever run in his life before. But the swooshing whooshing whiffling snorting noise was coming after him. Worse still, it was getting louder. This meant that the *thing*, the maker of the noise, the galloping creature, was getting closer. It was catching him up!

Run, Little Billy! Run run run!

He dodged around massive trees. He skipped over roots and brambles. He bent low to flash under

boughs and bushes. He had wings on his feet he ran so fast. But still the fearsome swooshing whooshing whiffling snorting noise grew louder and louder as it came closer and closer.

Little Billy glanced back quickly over his shoulder, and now, in the distance, he saw a sight that froze his blood and made icicles in his veins.

What he saw were two mighty puffs of orange-red smoke billowing and rolling through the trees in his

direction. These were followed by two more, *whoosh whoosh*, and then two more, *whoosh whoosh*, and they must surely be coming, Little Billy told himself, from the two nose-holes of some galloping panting beast that had smelled him out and was coming after him.

His mother's words began thrumming once again in his head:

Beware! Beware! The Forest of Sin!
None come out, but many go in!

'It's the Spittler for sure!' Little Billy cried out. 'Mummy said the Spittler blows smoke when it chases you. This one is blowing smoke! It's the Terrible Bloodsuckling Toothpluckling Stonechuckling Spittler! And soon it will catch me up and I'll be bloodsuckled and toothpluckled and stonechuckled and chewed up into tiny pieces, and then the Spittler will spit me out in a cloud of smoke and that will be the end of me!'

Woomph – Woomph!

Little Billy was running with the speed of an arrow, but each time he glanced back over his shoulder the puffs of orange-red smoky-breath had got closer. They were so close now he could feel the wind of them on the back of his neck. And the *noise*! It was deafening in his ears, this fearsome swooshing whooshing whiffling panting noise. *Woomph-woomph,* it went. *Woomph-woomph, woomph-woomph! Woomph-woomph!* It was like the noise made by a steam locomotive pulling out from a station.

Then suddenly he heard another noise that was somehow more fearsome still. It was the pounding of gigantic galloping hooves on the floor of the forest.

He glanced round again, but the Thing, the Beast, the Monster, or whatever it was, was hidden from his sight by the smoke it shot out as it galloped forward.

The smoky-breath was billowing all around him now. He could feel its hotness. Worse still, he could smell its smell. The smell was disgusting. It was the stench that comes from deep inside the tummy of a meat-eating animal.

'Mummy!' he cried out. 'Save me!'

Suddenly, directly in front of him, Little Billy saw the trunk of an enormous tree. This tree was different from the others because it had branches hanging down very low. While still running, he made a frantic jump for its lowest branch. He caught it and pulled himself up.

Then he grabbed the next branch above his head
and pulled himself up again. Then again and again,
climbing higher and higher to get away from the
terrible snorting, smoke-blowing, smelly-breathed
beast down below. He stopped climbing only when
he was too exhausted to climb any higher.

He looked up, but even now he couldn't see the top of the giant tree. It seemed to go on forever. He looked down. He couldn't see the ground either. He was in a world of green leaves and thick, smooth branches with no earth or sky in sight. The snorting smelly smoke-blowing beast was miles away down below somewhere. He couldn't even hear it any more.

Little Billy found a comfortable place where two big branches came together and he sat down to rest.

For the moment, at any rate, he was safe.

Then something very peculiar happened. There was a huge smooth branch very close to where Little Billy was sitting and he suddenly noticed that a small square patch of bark on this branch was beginning to move. It was a very small patch, about the size of a postage stamp, and the two sides of it seemed to be splitting down the middle and opening slowly outwards, like a pair of shutters on some tiny window.

Little Billy sat staring at this extraordinary thing. And all at once, a strange uncomfortable feeling came over him. It felt as though the tree he was sitting in and the green leaves all around him belonged to another world altogether and that he was a trespasser who had no right to be where he was. He watched intently as the tiny shutters of tree-bark opened wider and wider, and when they were fully open they revealed a small squarish window set neatly in the curve of the big branch. There was some sort of a yellowish glow coming from deep inside the window.

We Are the Minpins

The very next thing Little Billy saw was a tiny face at the window. It had appeared suddenly, from nowhere, and it was the face of an extremely old man with white hair. Little Billy could see this clearly despite the fact that the whole of the tiny man's head was no larger than a pea.

This ancient miniature face was staring straight at Little Billy with the most severe expression on it.

The skin on the face was deeply wrinkled all over, but the eyes were as bright as two stars.

Now something *even more* peculiar began to happen. All around him, not only on the huge main trunk of the tree but also on all the big branches that grew out of it, other tiny windows were opening

and tiny faces were peering out. Some of these faces belonged to men and others were clearly women. Here and there the head of a child was seen peering over a windowsill. The heads of these children were no larger than the heads of matchsticks. In the end, there must have been more than twenty small

windows all around where Little Billy was sitting, and from each window these amazing little faces were peering out. No sound came from any of the watchers.

The faces were silent, unmoving, almost ghost-like.

Now the tiny old man in the window nearest to Billy seemed to be saying something, but his voice was so soft and whispery, Little Billy had to lean right up close to catch his words.

'You're in a bit of a twizzler, aren't you?' the voice was saying. 'You can't go down again because if you do you'll be guzzled up at once. But you can't possibly sit up here forever, either.'

'I know, I know!' Little Billy gasped.

'Don't shout,' the tiny man said.

'I'm not shouting,' Little Billy said.

'Talk softer,' the tiny man said. 'If you talk too loud your voice will blow me away.'

'But . . . but . . . who *are* you?' Little Billy asked, taking care to speak very softly this time.

'We are the Minpins,' the tiny man said, 'and we own this wood. I shall come closer, then you will hear me better.' The old Minpin climbed out of his window and walked straight down the big steeply sloping branch, then up another branch until he found a place only a few inches from Little Billy's face.

It was amazing to see him walking up and down these almost vertical branches without the slightest trouble. It was like seeing someone walking up and down a wall.

'How on earth do you do that?' Little Billy asked.

'Suction-boots,' the Minpin said. 'We all wear them. You can't live in trees without suction-boots.' On his feet he was wearing tiny green boots rather like miniature wellies.

His clothes were curiously old-fashioned, mostly brown and black, the sort of thing people wore two or three hundred years ago.

Suddenly, all the other Minpins, men, women and children, were climbing out of their windows and making their way towards Little Billy. Their suction-boots seemed to allow them to walk up and down the steepest branches with the greatest ease, and some were even walking upside-down underneath

the branches. All of them were wearing these old-fashioned clothes from hundreds of years ago, and

several had on very peculiar hats and bonnets. They
stood or sat in groups on all the branches around

Little Billy, staring at him as though he were someone
from outer space.

'But do you all actually *live* inside this tree?' Little Billy asked.

The old Minpin said, 'All the trees in this forest are hollow. Not just this one, but *all* of them. And inside them thousands and thousands of Minpins are living. These great trees are filled with rooms and staircases, not just in the big main trunk but in most of the other branches as well. This is a Minpin forest. And it's not the only one in England.'

'Could I peep inside?' Little Billy said.

'Of course, of course,' the old Minpin said. 'Put your eye close to that window.' He pointed to the one he had just come out of.

Little Billy shifted his position and placed one eye right up against the square hole that was no bigger than a postage stamp.

What he now saw was quite marvellous.

The Gruncher Knows
You're Up Here

Little Billy saw a room that was lit by a pale
yellow light of some sort and it was furnished with
beautifully made miniature chairs and a table. To
one side was a four-poster bed. It was like one of
the rooms Little Billy had once seen in the Queen's
Doll's House at Windsor Castle.

'It's beautiful,' Little Billy said. 'Are they all as
lovely as this one?'

'Most are smaller,' the old Minpin said. 'This one is very grand because I am the Ruler of this tree. My name is Don Mini. What is yours?'

'Mine is Little Billy,' Little Billy said.

'Greetings, Little Billy,' Don Mini said. 'You are welcome to look into some of the other rooms if you wish. We are very proud of them.'

All the other Minpin families wanted to show Little Billy their own rooms. They rushed about along the branches calling out, 'Come and see mine! Please come and see mine!'

Little Billy began climbing about and peeping into the tiny windows.

Through one window he saw a bathroom, just like his own at home only a thousand times smaller. And through another he saw a classroom with lots of tiny desks and a blackboard at one end.

In every room there was a stairway in one corner leading up to the room above.

As Little Billy went from window to window, the Minpins followed him, clustering round and smiling at his exclamations of wonder.

'They're all absolutely marvellous,' he said. 'They're much nicer than our rooms at home.'

When the sightseeing tour was over, Little Billy sat down again on a large branch and said to the whole company of Minpins, 'Look, I've had a lovely time with you all, but how am I ever going to get home again? My mother'll be going crazy.'

'You can never get down from this tree,' Don Mini said. 'I've told you that. If you're stupid enough to try, you'll be eaten up in five seconds.'

'Is it the Spittler?' Little Billy asked. 'Is it the Terrible Bloodsuckling Toothpluckling Stonechuckling Spittler?'

'I've never heard of any Spittler,' Don Mini said. 'The one waiting for you down there is the fearsome Gruncher, the Red-Hot Smoke-Belching Gruncher. He grunches up everything in the forest. That's why we have to live up here. He has grunched up hundreds of humans and literally millions of Minpins. What makes him so dangerous is his amazing and magical nose. His nose can smell out a human or a Minpin or any other animal from ten miles away. Then he gallops towards it at terrific speed. He can never see anything in front of him because of all the smoke he belches out from his nose and mouth, but that doesn't bother him. His nose tells him exactly where to go.'

'Why does he blow out all that smoke?' Little Billy asked.

'Because he's got a red-hot fire in his belly,' Don Mini said. 'The Gruncher likes his meat roasted, and the fire roasts it as it goes down.'

'Look,' said Little Billy, 'Gruncher or no Gruncher, I've simply got to get home somehow. I'll have to make a dash for it.'

'Don't try it, I beg you,' Don Mini said. 'The Gruncher knows you're up here. He's down there now waiting for you. Climb down a bit lower with me and I'll show you.'

We Know All the Birds

Don Mini walked easily, straight down the side of the great tree-trunk. Little Billy climbed carefully after him, from one branch to the next.

Soon, below them, they began to smell the revolting hot stench of the Gruncher's breath, and the orange-red smoke was now billowing up into the lower branches in thick clouds.

'What does he look like?' Little Billy whispered.

'Nobody knows,' Don Mini answered. 'He makes so much steam and smoke you can never see him. If you are behind him you can sometimes catch a glimpse of little bits of him because all the smoke is being blown out in the front. Some Minpins say they have seen his back legs, huge and black and very hairy, shaped like lions' legs but ten times as big. And it is rumoured that his head is like an enormous crocodile's head, with rows and rows and rows of sharp pointed teeth. But nobody really knows. Mind you, he must have gigantic nose-holes to be able to blow out all that smoke.'

They stayed still, listening, and they could hear the Gruncher pawing the ground at the base of the tree with his giant hooves and snorting with greed.

'He smells you,' Don Mini said. 'He knows you aren't far away. He'll wait forever to get you now. He adores humans and he doesn't catch them very often. Humans are like strawberries and cream to him. You see, for months he's been living on a diet of Minpins, and a thousand Minpins is not even a snack for him. The brute is ravenous.'

Little Billy and Don Mini climbed back up the tree to where all the other Minpins were gathered. They seemed glad to see Little Billy come safely back.

'Stay up here with us,' they said to him. 'We'll look after you.'

Just then, a lovely blue swallow alighted on a branch not far away, and Little Billy saw a mother Minpin and her two children climb quite casually on to the swallow's back. Then the swallow took off and flew away with its passengers seated comfortably between its wings.

'Good Heavens!' cried Little Billy. 'Is that a special tame bird?'

'Not at all,' Don Mini said. 'We know all the birds.

The birds are our friends. We use them all the time for going places. That lady is taking her children to see their grandmother who lives in another forest about fifty miles away. They'll be there in less than an hour.'

'Can you *talk* to them?' Little Billy asked. 'To the birds, I mean?'

'Of course we can talk to them,' Don Mini said. 'We can summon them any time we want if we have to go somewhere. How else would we get our supplies of food up here? The Red-Hot Gruncher makes it impossible for us to walk anywhere in the wood.'

'Do the birds like doing this for you?' Little Billy asked.

'They'll do anything for us,' Don Mini said. 'They love us and we love them. We store food for them inside the trees so they don't starve when the icy-cold winter comes along.'

Suddenly all sorts of birds were alighting on the
branches of the tree around where Little Billy was
sitting, and the Minpins were climbing on to their
backs in droves. Most of the Minpins had small sacks
slung over their shoulders.

'At this time of day they go off to collect food,' Don Mini said. 'All the grown-ups have to help in getting food for the community. The population of each tree looks after itself. Our large trees are like your cities and towns, and the small trees are like your villages.'

It was an astonishing sight. Every kind of wonderful
bird was flying in and perching on the branches of
the great tree, and as soon as one landed a Minpin
would climb on to its back and off they would go.

There were blackbirds and thrushes and skylarks
and ravens and starlings and jays and magpies and
many kinds of small finches. It was all very fast and
well-organized. Each bird seemed to know exactly
which Minpin it was collecting, and each Minpin
knew exactly which bird he or she had ordered for
the morning.

'The birds are our cars,' Don Mini said to Little
Billy. 'They are much nicer and they never crash.'

Soon all the grown-up Minpins, excepting Don Mini, had flown away on birds and only the tiny children were left. Then the robins came in and the children began climbing on to their backs and going for short flights.

Don Mini said to Little Billy, 'The children all practise learning to fly on robins. Robins are sensible and careful birds and they love the little ones.'

Little Billy simply stood there staring. He could hardly believe what he was seeing.

CALL UP THE SWAN

While the children were practising on the robins, Little Billy said to Don Mini, 'Is there no way in the world to get rid of that disgusting Red-Hot Smoke-Belching Gruncher down below?'

'The only time a Gruncher dies,' Don Mini said, 'is if he falls into deep water. The water puts out the fire inside him and then he's dead. The fire to a Gruncher is like your heart is to you. Stop your heart and you die at once. Put out the fire and the Gruncher dies in five seconds. That's the only way to kill a Gruncher.'

'Now hang on a minute,' Little Billy said. 'Is there by any chance a pond or something around here?'

'There's a big lake on the far side of the forest,'

Don Mini said. 'But who's going to entice the Gruncher into that? Not us. And certainly not you. He'd be on you before you got within ten yards of him.'

'But you did say the Gruncher can't see in front of him because of all the clouds of smoke he blows,' Little Billy said.

'Quite true,' Don Mini said. 'But how is that going to help us? I don't think the Gruncher is ever going to fall into the lake. He never goes out of the forest.'

'I think I know how to make him fall in,' Little Billy said.

'What I want,' Little Billy went on, 'is a bird that is big enough to carry *me*.'

Don Mini thought about this for a while, then he said, 'You are a very small boy and because of that I think a swan could carry you quite easily.'

'Call up a swan,' Little Billy said. Suddenly there was a new authority in his voice.

'But . . . but I hope you're not going to do anything dangerous,' Don Mini cried.

'Listen carefully,' Little Billy said, 'because you must tell the swan exactly what he has to do. With me on his back he must fly down to the Gruncher. The Gruncher will smell me and know that I am very close. But he won't see me through all the steam and the smoke. He'll go mad trying to get at me. The swan will tantalize him by flying back and forth right in front of him. Is that possible?'

'Quite possible,' Don Mini said, 'except that you might easily fall off. You've had no flying practice at all.'

'I'll hang on somehow,' Little Billy said. 'Then the swan, keeping very low, will fly off through the forest with the ravenous Gruncher hotfoot in pursuit. The swan will keep just ahead of the Gruncher all the time, driving him crazy with my smell, and in the end the swan will fly straight over the big deep lake and the Gruncher, now travelling at terrific speed, will follow right behind. *Presto*, he's in the lake!'

'My boy!' Don Mini cried. 'You are a genius! Will you do it?'

'Call up the swan,' Little Billy ordered.

Don Mini turned to one of the robins which had just come back from a practice flight with a child Minpin on its back. Little Billy heard him talking to the robin in a kind of curious twitter. He couldn't understand a word of it. The robin nodded its head and flew off.

Two minutes later, a truly magnificent swan, as white as snow, came swooping in and landed on a branch nearby.

Don Mini walked over to it and once again a curious twittery conversation took place, a much longer one this time, with Don Mini doing nearly all the twittering and the swan nodding and nodding.

Then Don Mini turned to Little Billy and said, 'Swan thinks it's a great idea. He says he can do it. But he's just a bit anxious because you have never flown before. He says you must hang on very tight to his feathers.'

'Don't you worry about that,' Little Billy said. 'I'll hang on somehow. I don't want to be roasted alive and eaten by the Gruncher.'

Little Billy climbed on to Swan's back. Many of the Minpins who had flown away a short while before were now returning on their birds. Their tiny sacks were bulging. They stood around on the branches staring in wonder at the sight of this small human preparing to take off on Swan.

'Goodbye, Little Billy!' they called out. 'Good luck, good luck!' And with that, the great swan spread his wings and glided gently downward through the many branches of the big tree.

LITTLE BILLY HUNG ON TIGHT

Little Billy hung on tight. Oh, it was thrilling to be flying on the back of this great swan! It was wonderful to be up in the air and to feel the air swishing past his face. He hung on very tightly to Swan's feathers.

And suddenly, there it was just below them, the huge billow of orange-red smoke and steam coming from the nostrils of the awesome Gruncher. The smoke enveloped the beast completely, and yet through the smoke, as they got very close, Little Billy could just make out the enormous black shadow of some hairy monster. The snorting grew louder, and as the brute got more and more excited by the nearness of the delicious Little Billy smell, the smoke began coming out faster and faster, *whoomph-whoomph, whoomph-whoomph, whoomph-whoomph.* Little Billy could feel the monster getting closer, *whoomph-whoomph, whoomph-whoomph, whoomph-whoomph.*

Swan was flying back and forth right in front of the snorting cloud of smoke, tempting and tantalizing the beast and driving him mad with greed. The beast, or rather the cloud of smoke, kept lunging at Little Billy, but Swan was too quick for him and jinked away every time. The snorting grew louder and more ferocious every second, and the *whoomph-whoomphs* of thick hot steam came pouring out, thicker than ever.

Once, Swan looked round to see if Little Billy was all right. Little Billy nodded and smiled, and he could swear Swan nodded and smiled back at him.

At last, Swan must have decided they had done enough teasing. The great thick orange-red cloud was leaping up and down in a frenzy of hunger and desire, and the whole forest was echoing with the snorts and growls of the awesome creature. Swan glided round and headed in a straight line towards the edge of the forest, and of course the vast cloud of smoke came hurtling after him.

Swan was very careful to fly low all the time, keeping just in front of the Gruncher, leading him

on and on, threading a path carefully through the great trees in the forest. The scent of human food was very strong in the Gruncher's nostrils, and he must have been thinking that so long as he kept going flat out, he would catch his meal in the end.

Suddenly, right in front of them, on the edge of the forest, was the lake. The Gruncher, hurtling along right behind them, was interested only in the glorious human scent he was following.

Swan flew straight towards the lake. He skimmed low over the water. The Gruncher kept going.

Little Billy, looking back, saw the Gruncher plunging right into the lake, and then the whole lake seemed to erupt in a mass of boiling steaming frothing bubbling water.

For a brief moment, the terrible Red-Hot Smoke-Belching Gruncher made the lake boil and smoke like a volcano, then the fire went out and the awesome beast disappeared under the waves.

Hooray for Little Billy!

When it was all over, Swan and Little Billy flew higher and circled the lake for a last look.

And suddenly the whole sky around them was filled with birds, and every bird had one or more Minpins on its back. Little Billy recognized Don Mini riding on a fine jay and he was waving and cheering as he flew alongside them. It seemed that all the other Minpins from the big tree had turned up as well to witness the great victory over the dreaded Gruncher. Every kind of bird was circling around Little Billy and Swan, and the Minpins on their backs were waving and clapping and shouting with joy. Little Billy waved back and laughed and thought how wonderful it all was.

Then, led by Swan, all the birds and the Minpins returned to the home tree.

Back in the tree there was a tremendous celebration for Little Billy's victory over the dreaded Gruncher. Minpins from all over the forest had flown in on their birds to cheer the young hero, and all the branches and twigs of the great tree were crowded with tiny people. When the cheers and the clapping had died down at last, Don Mini stood up to make a speech.

'Minpins of the forest!' he cried, raising his small voice so that it could be heard all over the tree. 'The murderous Gruncher, who has gobbled up so many thousands of us Minpins, has gone forever!

The forest floor is safe at last for us to walk on! So now we can all go down to pick blackberries and winkleberries and puckleberries and muckleberries and twinkleberries and snozzberries to our heart's content. And our children can play among the wild flowers and the roots all day long.' Don Mini paused and turned his eyes upon Little Billy who was sitting on a branch not far away.

'But ladies and gentlemen,' he went on, 'who is it we have to thank for this great blessing that has come upon us? Who is the saviour of the Minpins?' Don Mini paused again. The Minpins in their thousands sat listening intently.

'Our saviour,' he cried out, 'our hero, our wonder-boy, is, as you already know, our human visitor, Little Billy.' (Cheers and shouts of 'Hooray for Little Billy!' from the crowd.)

Don Mini now turned and spoke directly to Little Billy. 'You, my boy, have done a wonderful thing for us and in return we wish to do something for you. I have had a word with Swan and he has agreed to become your personal private aeroplane for just as long as you remain small enough to fly on his back.' (More cheers and clapping and shouts of 'Good old Swan! What a great idea!')

'However,' Don Mini continued, still addressing Little Billy, 'you cannot go flying around all over the place on Swan's back in full daylight. Some human would be bound to see you. And then the secret would be out and you would be forced to tell your people all about us. That must never happen. If it did, crowds of enormous humans would come clumping all over our beloved forest to look for Minpins and our quiet homeland would be ruined.'

'I'll never tell a soul!' Little Billy cried out.

'Even so,' Don Mini said, 'we cannot risk you making daylight flights. But every night, after the light in your bedroom has been switched off, Swan will come to your window to see if you'd like a ride. Sometimes he will bring you back here to see us. Other times he will take you to visit places more wonderful than you could ever dream of. Would you like Swan to take you home now? I think we can risk just one more quick daylight flight.'

'Oh gosh!' Little Billy cried. 'I'd clean forgotten about home! Mummy'll be in a panic! I must fly!'

Don Mini gave the signal and in five seconds Swan swooped down and landed on the tree. Little Billy climbed on to his back, and as the great swan spread his wings and flew away, the whole forest, not just the tree they were in but the whole forest from end to end, came alive with the cheering of a million Minpins.

I Will Never Forget You!

Swan landed on the lawn of Little Billy's house, and Little Billy jumped off his back and ran to the living-room window. Very quietly he climbed in. The room was empty.

'Little Billy,' came his mother's voice from the kitchen. 'What are you up to in there? You've been very quiet for a long time.'

'I'm being good, Mummy,' Little Billy called back. 'I'm being very very good.'

His mother came into the room with a pile of ironing in her arms. She looked at Little Billy. 'What *have* you been doing?' she cried. 'Your clothes are absolutely filthy!'

'I've been climbing trees,' Little Billy said.

'I can't let you out of my sight for ten minutes,' his mother said. 'Which tree was it?'

'Just one of those old trees outside,' Little Billy said.

'If you're not careful you'll fall down and break an arm,' his mother said. 'Don't do it again.'

'I won't,' Little Billy said, smiling a little. 'I'll just fly up into the branches on silver wings.'

'What rubbish you talk,' his mother said and she walked out of the room with her ironing.

From then on, Swan came every night to Little Billy's bedroom window. He came after Billy's mother and father had gone to sleep and the whole house was quiet. But Little Billy was never asleep. He was always wide awake and eagerly waiting. And every night, before Swan arrived, he saw to it that the curtains were drawn back and the window was open wide so that the great white bird could come gliding right into the room and land on the floor beside his bed.

Then Little Billy would slip into his dressing gown and climb on to Swan's back and off they would go.

Oh, it was a wondrous secret life that Little Billy lived up there in the sky at night on Swan's back! They flew in a magical world of silence, swooping and gliding over the dark world below where all the earthly people were fast asleep in their beds.

Once, Swan flew higher than ever before and
they came to an enormous billowing cloud that
was shining in a pale golden light, and in the folds
of this cloud Little Billy could make out creatures
of some sort moving around.

Who were they?

He wanted so badly to ask Swan this question, but he couldn't speak a word of bird-language. Swan seemed unwilling to fly very close to these creatures from another world, and this made it impossible for Little Billy to see them clearly.

Another time, Swan flew through the night for what seemed like hours and hours until they came at last to a gigantic opening in the earth's surface, a sort of huge gaping hole in the ground, and Swan glided slowly round and round above this massive crater and then right down into it. Deeper and deeper they went into the dark hole.

Suddenly there was a brightness like sunlight below them, and Little Billy could see a vast lake of water, gloriously blue, and on the surface of the lake thousands of swans were swimming slowly about. The pure white of the swans against the blue of the water was very beautiful.

Little Billy wondered whether this was a secret meeting place of all the swans of the world, and he wished he had been able to ask Swan this question as well. But sometimes mysteries are more intriguing than explanations, and the swans on the blue lake, like the creatures on the golden cloud, would remain a mystery forever in Little Billy's memory.

About once a week, Swan would fly Little Billy back to the old tree in the forest to visit the Minpins. On one of these visits, Don Mini said to him, 'You are growing up fast, Little Billy. I'm afraid that soon you will be too heavy for Swan.'

'I know,' Little Billy said. 'I can't help it.'

'I'm afraid we don't have any bigger birds than Swan,' Don Mini said. 'But when he can't carry you any longer, I do hope you will still come up here to visit us.'

'I will, I will!' Little Billy cried. 'I will always keep coming to see you! I will never forget you!'

'And listen,' Don Mini said, smiling. 'Perhaps some of us might come down in great secrecy to visit *you*.'

'Could you really do that?' Little Billy asked.

'I think we might,' Don Mini said. 'We could trickle silently down to your house in the dark and creep into your bedroom for a midnight feast.'

'But how would you get all the way up to my bedroom window?' Little Billy asked.

'Have you forgotten our suction-boots?' Don Mini said. 'We'd simply walk straight up the wall of your house.'

'How lovely!' Little Billy cried. 'Then we can take it in turns visiting each other!'

'Of course we can,' Don Mini said.

And that is exactly what happened.

No child has ever had such an exciting young life as Little Billy, and no child has ever kept such a huge secret so faithfully. He never told a soul about the Minpins.

I myself have been very careful not to tell you where they live, and I am not about to tell you now. But if by some extraordinary chance you should one day wander into a forest and catch a glimpse of a Minpin, then hold your breath and thank your lucky stars because up to now, so far as I know, no one excepting Little Billy has ever seen one.

Watch the birds as they fly above your heads and, who knows, you might well spy a tiny creature riding high on the back of a swallow or a raven.

Watch the robin especially because it always flies low, and you might see a nervous young Minpin perched on the feathers having its first flying lesson.

And above all, watch with glittering eyes the whole world around you because the greatest secrets are always hidden in the most unlikely places.

Those who don't believe in magic will never find it.

NOTICE

It was nearly forty years ago that I first illustrated a book by Roald Dahl – *The Enormous Crocodile*. At the time I didn't realize that I was going to do many more, but, in fact, over the next twenty years I produced drawings for all of Roald Dahl's children's books.

All except one, that is. In 1990, at the same time as I was illustrating *Esio Trot*, the artist Patrick Benson was making large and beautiful pictures for *The Minpins*. I liked them very much, so perhaps you can imagine my surprise when, recently, I was asked to create a new set of illustrations for the book. The words in this new version are the same, but it is smaller and there are many more pages, so there is room for me to draw every single thing that happens. To do the drawings was very exciting for me, and it felt almost like a new Roald Dahl book that I had never read before. I hope you will feel the same.